Murder in
Ohiopyle
& Other Incidents

Written by
Marci Lynn McGuinness

Shore Publications

Murder in Ohiopyle and Other Incidents
by Marci Lynn McGuinness

Published by Shore Publications
P. O. Box 74, Ohiopyle, PA 15470
www.ohiopyle.info
443-480-3730

First Edition published under name of *Incidents* © 1992
Second Edition, *Murder in Ohiopyle and Other Incidents*, © Marci
McGuinness, 2009. All rights reserved.

Printed in the United States of America

Cover Photographs by Marci McGuinness.
Background photo: Ohiopyle Falls in High Water, May 2009.
Inset Photo: Ohiopyle Grant & Lincoln Street dumpster,
August 2009.

For feedback on this title or other Marci McGuinness/Shore
Publications titles, contact: marci@ohiopyle.info. Order all
Marci McGuinness/Shore Publications titles at:
www.ohiopyle.info or www.amazon.com.

Life is a mystery
That much we know
From birth to death
We all must go

Marci McGuinness

Introduction

Marci McGuinness has brought to you her original fiction. The author is best known for her series of vintage photograph "Yesteryear" books. Although she loves researching local history, recording and preserving the old stories and memories, she has been writing fiction since she was 6 years old. Look for her novel, *Murder in St. Michaels,* in 2010.

Contents

Murder in Ohiopyle   7

A Song for Lester   21

His Mistake   27

Natural Revenge   31

Ghostly   35

No Such Thing as Security   41

Makin' Change   45

The Town Pest   59

Cautious Encounter   65

Poor Harry   69

Late Bloomin'   73

Nobody's Child   79

The Killjoy Cookie   85

Murder in Ohiopyle

Solace is a funny thing. God will only allow you so much of it before throwing some action your way. I had hidden in my house all weekend with a few good books, taking naps and watching movies. On the way to the Post Office this Tuesday morning I thought my Jack Russell, Jack, was bothering the fellow on the bench. He was just ahead of me on Grant Street in Ohiopyle.

"Come on," I summoned. He ignored me and sniffed the man further.

I did not have my glasses on, so I could not see more than 10 feet in front of me. I jogged over and started to smile at the man. His head was hanging a bit and I thought, at first, that he was sleeping. I realized it was Herman Cranker so I touched the Ohiopyle Councilman's cap, then his shoulder, "Herman, are you okay?"

It was 7 AM, the day after Labor Day. Most years, this is my favorite day in Ohiopyle. The tourists and transient river workers are gone. It is exquisitely quiet. Herman did not respond. Nothing. I sat next to him and took his wrist. No pulse.

"Crap!"

Jack was dancing around and barking at me, at Herman. I said my good byes to a man I knew all my life. He was 89, had seemed 89 to me for 40 years. It was when I stood up that I realized blood was trickling out of his ear on the other side of his head. I have watched enough *Perry Mason, Matlock, Murder She Wrote* and *Law & Order* to know what that meant. Who would hurt the old man? I called 911 and then took pictures of Herman from several angles with my camera phone.

It was then that I realized that someone was angry with the grouchy, opinionated man at any given moment. This may be real difficult to figure out. He upset folks at the council meetings each month and wrote letters to the editor regularly, stirring things up. I also realized that if someone else came by and messed with him, that would be bad, too, so I stayed there and left a friend a message.

"Frank, someone killed old Herman Cranker from here in the borough. I found him on a bench and will send you photos as soon as I get off the phone. He is on the bench just past the dumpster at the corner of Grant and Lincoln, bleeding out of his ear. Looks like a gash from a rock. I don't know how or why, but he is sure gone."

Jack sat next to Herman's leg, whining an almost imperceptible cry.

I shook my head while trying to catch my breath. I was dizzy, but knelt down and took a few very deep breaths, before looking around to see if there was anyone at all in the woods or the town watching me. I have always heard criminals love to do that.

There would be tons of people arriving very soon, so if I wanted to figure out anything from the scene, I thought I had better start paying close attention to detail. The dumpster next to him was not only overflowing, but garbage was stacked all around it on the ground and on top of it. I wanted to move Herman away from the filth and thanked God the bulk of the tourist season was over. A group of bicyclists and the Post Master showed up just before the Park Rangers, firemen, and then, the State Police.

Four men and a young girl and her mom on a bicycle built for two tried to gather around. They were shooed away. It was 68 degrees now. The wind was calm. It would be good to get him out of here before the flies and bees from the trash found him.

Sirens wailed and men in uniform could be seen coming our way from all directions. At this very place, just yesterday, parents watched their children play on the swings adjacent. People picnicked. They laughed and littered profusely from the bench. Now, this. Looking around, the sky was a gorgeous blue, a few bicycles passed us by, slowing and staring. I said a silent prayer for Herman and shook the Park Manager's hand.

"Hi, Cane. I found him like this maybe 20 seconds before I called you. Actually, Jack found him."

He smiled at Jack, who looks like a white wiener dog (don't tell him), sighed, and looked at me. "You okay, Mayor?"

"Not my usual morning, but yeah. Creepy to think someone cracked the old man in the head and ran." We shared a look, looked around.

A Pennsylvania State Policeman touched my elbow and I turned. "Ma'am," he nodded.

"Please don't call me Ma'am, Sir, uh, Officer, I mean," I grinned.

He and Cane shook hands, exchanged nods.

"This is Mayor Mitchum," Cane said, backing away.

He was a big handsome fellow who nodded with a smile. "I am Officer Paul Watkins. I believe you found the man and made the call."

I nodded agreement.

"Could you step over here and tell me what happened?"

I followed him the few steps noticing his fine physique. He was holding a writing pad and began.

"Why don't you start from the beginning and try to tell me every detail you can remember? Even a small thing that seems unimportant could turn out to be vital to the investigation."

I looked at the sky, but God was leaving this up to me. "I was walking pretty fast when I saw Jack..."

9

"Hi, Jack," he said to the little old dog who was wagging his tail at him.

"I saw Jack sniffing a man on the bench there. Without my glasses, I can't see far, so I couldn't tell who it was until I got closer. I called to him, but he kept sniffing. Once I could see it was Herman Cranker, I thought he was sleeping. His head was nodded forward a little. He is old. It would not surprise me if an 89 year old man fell asleep on this otherwise peaceful bench."

"Yeah," he agreed.

"Anyway, Jack ignored me and kept whining and circling him. I tapped his cap. It was hard to see his face, leaned over with the cap hiding it. Then I touched his shoulder. He didn't respond. I sat down next to him and took his wrist, no pulse. I sat there for a few seconds, a little dizzy from the shock of finding a dead man who I have known all my life."

I breathed deeply, leaning with my hands on my knees.

"Take your time. You okay?" he asked.

I stood and continued breathing deeply, looking back at Herman. Yellow crime scene tape was going up. He would soon be moved. There were actually detectives there in suits…just like TV.

"They are quick," I thought aloud.

He nodded. "Then what happened?"

"Then, as I got up, I noticed blood trickling from his ear." I leaned down again, dizzy.

"I'm okay." I stood. "I looked closer and saw he had a gash. That's when I thought I would puke, but got it together and called 911."

"Did you see anyone?"

"There was no one around that I noticed. Um. A car passed us on our way here, though."

"Who?"

"Herman's next door neighbor, Ike Landing. They used to walk together until Ike's knees gave out."

10

We looked at each other.

"No way. He was probably sitting there complaining about the garbage, drinking coffee." I said.

"Anything else? Anything unusual?"

"Hmm. I don't always pay attention. There are normally a lot of people around so I ignore a lot. I need to let my mind settle." I rolled my shoulders and neck. Jack was jumping against my leg, yelping. I picked him up. Officer Watkins scratched his ears.

"I am thinking," I offered as we locked eyes. "I need a drink of water and a seat."

"I have water. Let's walk over to my car, Mayor."

He pointed to his unmarked car. He stepped aside so I could lead. We walked by the scene. I watched as they finished up with Herman and readied him to be moved. Jack whined when they removed the old man's John Deere® cap. I knew he had squabbles with people, but who would kill him out here? He was alone. He had no children. Could Ike really have done that? I knew he didn't have the strength or the will to kill his only real friend.

I could hear the Youghiogheny River and falls flowing by just a block and a half below us. Ohiopyle is the scene of a murder, I thought. I tried to force myself to understand this was really going on. I had not run across any reported murders in the borough's history. Growing up, "Mountain Justice" was implied if people were beat up or disappeared. It wasn't talked about. My mind wandered.

"Earth to, oh, I did not get your full name."

"Recca Mitchum." I watched his face. They always have some wise comment about my name. This would be interesting.

"Recca?" he asked, handing me a cold bottled water from his soft-pack cooler.

"Yes," I smiled. He got points for no sarcasm.

We watched as the men passed us, preparing to take Herman Cranker away from Ohiopyle forever. Everyone who knew him thought he would die in his neglected house long before anyone discovered him.

"No one liked him except his neighbor, Ike," I said matter-of-factly.

"How about you? How did you feel about him?"

"Do you suspect that I picked up a rock and slammed that old fart in the head with it before breakfast this morning?"

"No, I don't." he said.

"Lord! Okay. He was always very old to me. I paid little attention to him. He grunted at me all my life. I took that as a "Hello" and always spoke to him. He married a local girl who passed away in childbirth years ago. He used to work for the Western Maryland Railroad. I know little else about him except that he liked to fight with people on the town council. That is what he was known for-his strong opinions and non-compromising ways."

"How did you handle him as an unruly type councilman?"

"With very thick kid gloves."

"Oh. Anything else?"

"Yes, it makes me sick that anyone could get killed here. This is paradise. I'd like to crack that person in the head." My gaze caught the dumpster. "And whoever is responsible for that!"

He looked at me flatly. "Don't worry. I understand and won't include that last statement in the report. Can you read and sign your statement? I will need your home address and phone number...unless there is more?"

I have dealt with a few cops in my life and local ones have rarely impressed me. I do however, love New York City cops, but he was waiting for an answer.

"I am starved. Come on Jack," I said as I smiled, nodded and headed down the road toward home, hoping to escape the insanity the morning turned into (and the media).

There were more law enforcement cars gathered than I have

ever seen in Ohiopyle altogether in my lifetime. Reporters and photographers were clamoring for a look. My friend, Frank, photographer for the local newspaper walked toward me, waving. "I got the shots. Are you alright?" he asked.

"Numb, dizzy. How are you? Do I need to tell the cops I sent those to you? I forgot about that."

"Sure, they'll want to have them. I am going to need your story before all these hounds get to you. If you think you want to have lunch, I'll be around here a while."

"I am starved." I said as Jack and I turned back to find Officer Watkins.

I caught his eye and pointed for him to meet me over on a rock I had every intention of sitting on. Jack jumped into my lap as he approached us. At this point adrenaline had me wrapped so tight I could barely think. The dizziness wasn't letting up.

"I forgot," I said as I opened the photos on my phone. His eyes popped. I grinned at him. "Took them before anyone else touched him, ya know?"

"Wise. I'll have to take your phone as evidence."

I looked at him a moment, enjoying the scenery of his well-crafted face, before having to delve into a subject that may upset him. Mad policemen are no one's favorite people.

"I had already sent the photos to Frank before meeting you." I pointed in his direction.

Officer Watkins flagged Frank our way while frowning at me. "Publishing the photos may help in some way," I suggested.

I believe cops need help sometimes and I wasn't personally comfortable leaving everything up to them. I worried they would just let it go after a while, unsolved, or put their own political spin on it. I was not young and have seen some games played.

The daily paper hit our porch at 6 AM . I was nervous while

unfolding it to see the front page. The headline jumped out at me. "Ohiopyle Councilman Murdered." Jack popped his head up when I gasped. Seeing that in print knocked the air out of me. I thought I was getting my emotions settled after a pretty good night's sleep, but I was whirling again.

Jack got up, stretched and came out on the porch, growling. "What is it?" I asked as I followed his gaze.

What looked like a bloody energy drink can sat in the rocking chair. It rocked as Jake grabbed the can. He tried to bite me when I wrestled it out of his mouth. If this was evidence, it sure is compromised now was all I could think when Officer Watkins pulled up in his unmarked car.

"Good Morning. What do you have there?" He got out of the car as she held it out.

"I just came out to get the paper."

He glared at me. "That was why I stopped by. I was afraid for you."

"Well, Jack growled and I turned and saw this can on the rocking chair. It looks like there may be blood on it. Jack sure acts like it is. Before I could stop him, he snatched it up. I wrestled it from him. It also could just be litter. It is everywhere here especially after a holiday weekend."

He brought a plastic bag from his pocket and had me drop it gently into it.

"Is there a note?"

"A note?"

"With the can. Was there a note left?"

"That would be just a bit too handy, wouldn't it?"

He shrugged and went over the area. Now my porch is a crime scene, I thought.

"I suppose this makes me look even guiltier. You better get this guy before I do or he is going to be crying for his mother."

"Do not interfere with this, Recca. Besides the legalities, you could easily get hurt or get others hurt. Do you understand?"

"Of course I understand." I took Jack in the house and washed my hands. He was still there when I returned, so I just sat on the swing and let out a sigh. "Go ahead and say what you came to say, before the can incident."

"This is not a game. A killer is free to roam. Free to kill. You are a target in case you do not get the message he or she is sending you."

"I said that I understand."

We stared at each other. Someone not only killed Herman, but thinks they can waltz onto our porch and leave bloody threats. I understood alright. The words "God help him" rolled through my mind.

"I understand you are wasting precious time sitting here staring at me."

"I have a feeling I can't leave you without your doing something foolish."

"I am starved," I said as I walked into the house with the newspaper and waved good bye. He smiled as I closed the door.

He knocked on the door. I opened it.

"I need your cooperation. I do not want to have to stop you from proceeding with your own investigation."

"You assume a lot. I just got up. I had a particularly tough day yesterday and this day is not looking good thus far. Go investigate and get back to me real quick cause I want to meet this coward."

"I will be keeping in touch."

"I don't suppose you can tell me what Ike had to say?"

He shook his head back and forth.

I smiled, closed the door, sat on the floor and cried. Jack licked my face, after licking his butt I am sure, and curled up in my lap. I started to settle down and breathed deeply. I sat up, stretched, looked out at the old wicker rocker, swore profusely and went to the kitchen.

After a huge breakfast of home fries, scrambled eggs and

15

spinach, coffee and toast, I put Jack on the leash and ran to
Herman's bench. This is what people were already calling it.
Herman's Bench. I stepped over the yellow tape and sat
where I had sat next to the old man the day before. I looked
around at every detail of the woods, the people. I wondered
if this person was watching me. In case, I stood and flipped
him off in all directions. I smiled at the people who saw me. I
have lived here all my life and decided that this person
probably knows this and may follow me. They didn't, but I
took a great hike that did me a lot of good. While walking, I
hoped to meet up with this person and feed him to the bears,
but the chance did not arise.

On the way back home I tied Jack outside and went into Falls
Market. The place was full of customers. I sat down with Ike
and a couple other locals and ordered a big water and some
chili cheese fries. I know I ate earlier, but I was starved.

One man thought that Herman must have fallen and hit his
head just as Ike left him, then sat up on the bench to rest and
died there. They didn't know about the bloody can and I
didn't tell them. I figured this idiot was seeking attention and
I was not priming the pump for him. Let him wander.

Ike looked at me intently and tapped my hand under the
table. After he left to go home, I got Jack and followed him
as I felt he wanted me to do. I went around to his back door.
It was a well-kept private yard and porch. That is where I
found him.

"What is going on, Ike?"

He handed me a memory card.

"Do you know what this is?"

"It is a memory card. Maybe you need to tell me something
the cops don't know about."

"I don't mean to hold out on 'em. I miss him already.
Herman was my only friend."

"When I saw you yesterday morning, you must have just left
him."

16

"Yes. He was dying when I got there. He put this in my hand. Squeezed it hard into it, said what I think was the word "news," and died. I got scared and went home, but I am not sure what he gave me. Is it important?"

I ran home to retrieve my laptop computer. We looked at the pictures and short videos of one litterbug after another. It seemed Herman was photographing them and by the looks on many of their faces, oftentimes, harassing them. There were parents, children, river workers, and people of all ages and walks of life throwing litter on the ground next to the playground dumpster in Ohiopyle. There were hundreds of photos all taken since May this year. The last one was taken just minutes before either Ike or I saw Herman that morning.

My phone rang and brought us out of the shock we were in. "Are you onto this nut yet cause if they can just kill an old man in the middle of Ohiopyle, they must be a freaking ghost or something," I said before Officer Watkins could speak.
"Calm down, now. I am coming to pick you up in 2 hours. Be there and packed."
He hung up before I could tell him to go leap over the falls in high water.
"Ike, can you hold on to this memory card a bit longer?" I handed it to him when I got it out of the computer.
I grabbed my truck keys and Jack and headed out the door. Jack stood on my lap as we pulled around behind the house. He was so alert his vibes could have powered Ohiopyle during peak season. Mine, too, I'm sure. I knew Jack would let me know if I did not hear or feel someone coming, so I tried to let my mind relax in order to come up with some answers. I wondered just what Herman intend ed doing with the photos. He often sent scenic Ohiopyle photos to the newspaper, and they published many.

17

Was it a planned killing or did he get smart with the wrong person yesterday and get nailed? And why the bloody can on the rocker? Why would anyone want to scare me? I hadn't done anything but find him. The whole town knew his morning schedule and most everyone I knew had something against him at some point throughout their lives. I didn't. Neither did Ike.

Jack looked up and let out a low guttural growl the likes of which I had never heard. A coyote was on the steps outside the screened porch, a small turkey in its mouth. I took a deep breath and sprayed it in the eyes with the extremely hot pepper spray I brought along. It squealed and took off, but never dropped the turkey.

Jack was barking insanely when I turned around and she hit me in he temple with something I thought was a camera. I could hear Jack tearing at her and her swearing, but my head rang and I couldn't see for a minute. She was on me in the front seat of the old Ford, choking me when I got a grasp on the hammer.

I starting hitting her body with it best I could but she strangled most of the strength out of me. She is not small, Mrs. Leafing. Jack must have nailed her a good one because I was able to finally catch a breath and swung with all my might. Blood exploded from her head just as I heard Officer Watkins' voice. I shoved her off of me onto the passenger side floor and kind of back flipped/rolled out onto the ground. Jack kept ripping into her. A young officer tried to get him off the council-woman.

Officer Watkins gently grabbed hold of me in a way I kind of liked.

"She could have killed you," he said.

I stared at him, sure blood was splattered over every inch of my face. A woman lay bleeding, but I swear he was about to kiss me when I turned to take Jack from the young officer who held him out trying to keep from getting bit.

I found out that the widow Leafing and old Herman were
special friends for years until he saw her littering by that
dumpster one day. According to what she had said while
choking me, he would not forgive her. Evidence found in his
home showed the dumpster became his obsession. He had
planned to publish a book of all the litterbug photos to
distribute free. He also had plans to air the videos online and
had already posted dozens of the photos to several popular
social web sites. It seems this really set Mrs. Leafing off.
Ike fought for custody of Herman's ashes and sprinkled them
around his bench. Officer Watkins has been calling, but I let
it go to voice mail. My father always warned me against
kissing cops or lawyers. He was a county judge. He knew.

A Song for Lester

Being a street person was getting to Lester today. It would not be so bad if he only had someone to talk to. The Community Center buzzed with activity and haggling. He sold things here at the weekend flea market regularly. Some things he found in the trash and others on people who rubbed too closely to him on the crowded city streets. You could rent a table for a few dollars. After bumming his table rent from the theater goers Saturday night he crawled into a culvert below the new bridge for a good night's sleep. Now he was at the Sunday sale feeling lonely and ignored.

It had been a while since his last good scrubbing and it showed in appearance and aroma. Ladies cackled about their bake sales and handmade quilts. Old men sold their tools and car parts. He sold only one gold chain so far and could not get his desired price. He wished he was back home in the mountains on his mother's front porch.

When Lester Abbot left his mountain home for the city he had big dreams. Most of them had come true, but it was painfully obvious to the once handsome, energetic man that the good life does not always last. His wife had run up enormous bills without his knowledge. Bills he was not aware of until the sheriff came to his home and posted it for sale. Even the healthy income that he took in could not cover her extensive debts. His home was sold along with the contents to pay off the remaining bills.

After taking to the bottle, Lester lost his job at the cosmetics company he had managed for a decade. He rented a room at a boarding house but always drank up his money and was evicted. Lester had lived on the streets of Pittsburgh for six years now. He had no real friends or family since burying his folks long ago. His fondest memories were of summer evenings on the front porch singing with his dad who played the banjo. He wanted to feel like singing again.

The day of the Sheriff's Sale, his wife, Lola, took his son and his car and never got in touch with him again. He remembered singing "I'm a Yankee Doodle Dandy" with Toby while bathing him the night before he last saw him. "How much for the watch?" the teenage girl asked him, bringing him out of his thoughts.

"Forty bucks," he barked, straightening his bony frame in the crooked folding chair.

Her pink spiked hair brought a smile to Lester's face until he saw her swollen belly. He actually pitied the girl's situation and gave her a small break on the watch. As she waddled away, Lester found himself enjoying the sight of her soft body. He had refused to let himself even think about women for all these years. The scars that Lola left ran deep. He had loved her with all his heart but now dreamed only of reuniting with his son. He realized the time had come for him to start growing again. He had to somehow build a decent life, find his son and return to the mountains. The ways of the city had turned him into an old man before his time.

Looking into the mirror next to him he could hardly believe the reflection was that of Lester Abbot. His baggy drab trousers were thick and hard from grime. They had not been washed since he found them in the trash more than a year ago. His only possessions were being sold at this rusty card table. It sickened him to think of the turn his life had taken. His poverty and filth embarrassed him. He dreamed of becoming a clean cut man who commanded respect.

His thoughts kept him from hustling the passersby for sales. He had only taken in enough money to get a room for a couple nights. He had made up his mind to stay sober and devise a plan to get off the cold dangerous streets for good. Twice he had been stabbed for his bottle but lately the urge to drink had been dwindling.   The loud talk of the ladies near him brought his mind back to the flea market. The big blonde with red lip stick was saying something about a woman named Lola.

"She thinks her stuff don't stink but I know better. She's been humpin' the boss since day one," she yelled to the older Italian woman across the aisle. 'Ain't right the way she lets that kid run the streets either."
Lester sat back and looked at the blonde lady who sold ceramic animals of all sizes and colors.
He had to ask, "What's Lola's last name?"
The big lady looked at him as if he were crazy to be speaking to her.
"Her name. Lola who?"
"I can't tell you that," she said in a raspy whisper.

Lester rose form his seat and moved toward her, shuffling his ragged sneakers. She stood steadfast seeming to hold her breath. He looked her sternly in the eyes.
"Abbot," she said softly.
"Where do you work?" he commanded.
"The dry cleaners on the corner of Center and First."

He walked back to the table and gathered his things. His legs took him to First Street and south toward Center to find a room close to Lola's employment.
At the Penn Hotel he took a bath. A luxury he had not had in a while. He soaked in the claw foot tub and smoked a cigar in celebration of his findings. Tomorrow he would see his wife and son.
Delbert's Dry Cleaners was bustling at noon when Lester ventured down to take a look. Lola came out of the front entrance with a huge man on her arm. Lester had to admit she looked pretty good. Earlier that morning he had gone to the Goodwill Thrift Store and bought two new

outfits. He felt better about himself than he had in years. Following the couple into a diner, he pulled his hat over his eyes and took the booth behind theirs.

While listening to the pair coo and kiss, he ordered coffee. The waitress had just brought their "usual" when he got up the nerve to approach them.

"Spare change?" he mumbled to the heavy man who sat there holding his estranged wife's hand.
"Yeah, hold on." The man searched deep into his pockets and came up with a handful of coins. "A laundry man always has change," he boasted and dropped the silver in a pile by his plate. Lester rummaged in the pile until a quarter rolled toward Lola. Their eyes met. The little wrinkles at the sides of her blue eyes pointed upward with the questioning look her face took on.

"Lester," she gasped with realization.

"We have to talk," was all he could muster.

"You know this guy, honey?" the large man asked.

"Yeah. He's a relative. I'll talk to him. Just be a minute." Her voice broke trying to come to grips with this surprise meeting with the husband she robbed and deserted so long ago.

They say across from each other in his booth. He waited for her to speak.

"How have you been Lester?" she asked slowly without meeting his eyes.

"How could you have done this to me?" he whispered with a hateful passion.

Lola dried the tears in her overly made-up eyes. "I have always felt awful about leaving you but there was no other way," she pleaded.

"I can't believe you were right here all the time. I didn't know how to start looking or where."

"Now you found me, so what do you want?"

24

"Toby."

"Forget it!" she screamed, spitting all over him. "You can't have my son," she insisted, pounding a limp wrist on the Formica tabletop.

"You stole him from me!"

Lola leaned against the back of the booth. Her dark hair was sprayed so stiff he had to fight the urge to jump up and make a mess of it.

"What if I refuse to let you see him?"

"I'll kill you," he told her.

Lola stared at her husband. She began to realize this was not the easy-going wimp she had married. The look in his eyes told her he was not bluffing.

"Toby is no little boy. He may not accept you."

"I'm his father. He should know the truth!"

"He thinks you didn't want to come with us when the house was sold."

"And now you have fat boy payin' your bills."

"Looks to me like you gave up your three-piece suit," she said ignoring his comment.

"I gave up a lot of things. A dry cleaner's whore ain't exactly the big time!" he said using tremendous self-control to keep from belting her.

Just then a handsome boy entered the diner. "Mom, I knew you'd be here. I need some money for a pizza party at Jimmy's after school."

He eyed the man sitting across from his mother and knew. "Dad?" he mumbled.

"Hello, Son," Lester said through the knot forming in his throat.

"Your father had a hard time finding us," Lola said.

"I'll say," he sulked.

"Your mother never let me know where you were,

Toby. I've missed you."

The boy watched his father while talking to his mother. "Can I have the money, Mom? Jimmy's outside waitin' for me."

While Lola dug into her purse Lester handed the boy his last ten dollar bill. "Have fun," he said.

"Thanks...Dad," he hesitated, backing out of the diner keeping his eyes on this man he remembered as his Dad.

"You can't buy his love," Lola said flatly.

"Don't worry," he said. "There's no chance of that."

Lester got up and walked away from her, an unfamiliar bounce to his step. He began singing "I'm a Yankee Doodle Dandy" out on the sidewalk as he watched his son turn the corner of Center.

His Mistake

You know how life is. How things happen in sequence so fast sometimes that it amazes everyone around. That's how it was after Dirt opened his big mouth to the wrong woman. His world was never the same.

First of all, let me explain that Dirt Fagly was not well liked. He was tolerated by many for reasons I can not imagine, but he had the respect of no one, unlike Marti, the lady he thought he had pegged as a morally loose woman who had no one who cared. That was his mistake.

So Marti and her friend just had dinner at what is a well-known restaurant around the mountains where they lived. They both worked hard and raised families and once in a while went out for a break. They had a delicious dinner and went to the lounge for a drink with friends who were also dining there. They talked and laughed and played the juke box. The place was rather busy for a week night, and it was getting late. They decided to leave after they finished their drink.

Along came Dirt, who, by the way, was with his wife. He asked Pat about her new baby, as if he cared. He then turned to Marti and said, "What is it with you anyway? Can't you at least say 'Hi, how are you, Dirt?' You never speak to us," he said, meaning him and his wife.

Marti, being who she is, laughed and said, "I didn't know we were buddies."

That was it. He lost it. In his mind he thought he had a right to be standing there verbally assaulting this woman. He called her a whore and a lesbian. He could not figure which. She was beautiful and intelligent that, anyone who really knew her, knew for sure. He threatened to throw her through the plate glass window and Pat jumped in his face telling him what an idiot he was. She would not let Marti crack him in the mouth. She was hollering for the bartender, who came, in many's opinion, too late. Pat was hysterical and Marti pushed her out the door. She knew the guy was insignificant and did not really want to crack him or touch his greasy being in any way.

"He has to be him the rest of his life, that's his worse punishment of all," Marti told her friend.

Pat was fuming about none of the men in the bar stopping him from going on and on - and letting him threaten her friend. She was right, but Marti told her they were wimps and could not help it. It was not surprising to her, although it hurt.

Like I told you, things happen in life. And this began a chain of events that no one could have anticipated. The bartender, I hear, clued old Dirt in on who he had messed with. He realized Dirt was in very serious danger if Marti chose to tell this story to her powerful family members. But Marti was wise. She sent him a book on etiquette and decided if he ever spoke to her again in that manner she would go ahead and break his nose and knees. She let if go for the time being.

But the bar had been crowded that night, and word got around to all sorts of people, none of whom liked Dirt much and many who respected Marti. First he got threatening phone calls - was told to watch his back. Then his vehicle blew up in his driveway. Copperhead snakes appeared in his hot tub. That tacky wife of his passed out from the sight of them. Then when I heard their dog was missing, I knew who it was. Marti's family has been here a long time. They have helped a lot of people and some have strong feelings for them. Too bad for Dirt.

His wife was always home laying around talking on the phone to whoever would listen. I can picture them watching her through the window and getting all frothy at the mouth. It would make a good movie. Anyhow. She was the next to come up missing. At first Dirt thought she left him.

But she took no money. That was not like her.

Now, naturally, the police got in on this, and Dirt blamed Marti and her clan, who all to his dismay, had alibis. He claimed they had paid someone to do it. But the police knew them. That was not their style. They were baffled and gave Marti hell for not telling them about the incident in the first place. She believed in karma. That everything works out. She was right. The wife never returned. No one expected her. Dirt wanted to harass Marti but wanted to live more. Life went on.

Months later he received a photograph. It was her. She was skinny and filthy and the look in her eyes was blank. The look of one who is catatonic. Scared into oblivion. On the back of it were two words.

"Yu nicst."

They were almost unreadable. Written by a child, it seemed.   It was obvious enough that it meant Dirt was next. He was frantic. Emotionally shot. He already looked and acted like someone else. The arrogance was long gone. His eyes were bugged out. He could not eat. This was the first real clue the police had. They knew she was taken by at least one illiterate. But when you get back into these hills there is a bit of that. The cops had no intentions of going to every shanty in every hollow to question people. They had made that mistake before. They did not like the Fagly's much either and put very little effort into the case after that. When Dirt finally came up missing no one noticed. What friends he had before stayed away from him. They liked living and realized there was something bigger than them at work here.

In her heart Marty knew who had taken them and what had been done. When she passed the end of the lane she always wanted to check the large cooler that sat up on posts. People say they kept snakes in there. Maybe they used to.

Natural Revenge

Managing the Country Club meant long hours for Marge Logan. The thirty mile ride to her mountain home often frightened her and got her imagination to working overtime. What would she do if she broke down at 3 a.m. on a Sunday morning? Walking to a stranger's house and waking them to use the phone was not her idea of fun. She was always so relieved to pull into her driveway safe and sound. The late rides were nerve wracking, but she never gave a thought to quitting her job or changing careers. The scary nights were just a small flaw in a life she thoroughly enjoyed.

Marge was a wonder woman of the nineties juggling career, marriage, children and household duties. Everything seemed to be going smoothly. The kids were all finally in school. Her marriage was strong and fun. They were even taking a family vacation each summer with a little left to put in their savings. The Logans were happy.

She asked the bartender to close up the club in hopes of getting home before midnight for once.

The headlights crossed her lane on top of Summit Mountain. She laid on the horn while cutting the wheel to the right. His Chevy hit her Ford with full force at the driver's door. Marge was spun downhill until her vehicle collided with an embankment. She was pinned in her seatbelt, therefore taking the entire impact to her small frame. "Dead on arrival," they told her husband. The driver of the Chevy had been blind drunk but uninjured. There were large amounts of cocaine in his system. He was known around town as a wealthy spoiled party animal.

Alex Logan was sitting up with Tammy, 9, Alice, 7, and Bruce, 6, watching the late show when they received the news about the wife and mother they loved and depended on. They were sick with shock and grief. They huddled together crying hysterically on the new sofa Marge had just charged on the Sears card. After a few moments of this Alex dried his eyes and told them to listen carefully, "I have to go to the police to identify your mother," he began slowly. "You will have to go over to Gramma's.

"We're stayin' with you," Tammy insisted. They piled into their father's work truck clinging to each other in desperation. As they followed the police car the only sound coming from the Logan truck was the banging of the ladder in the bed. Alex was a construction worker. He built houses, office buildings, home additions, garages, and whatever else needed built. Bruce was the first to break what had come to be an unbearable silence.

"Mom can't be de de dead," he croaked.

"I wish that were true, Son," Alex whispered. The lump in his throat seemed to expand and cause his whole head to throb. "We have to be strong and stick together. We'll be OK," he tried to assure them.

Alice was their middle child who looked and spoke just like Marge. "It's all right. Mom is in heaven with Grandpa. She is watching us."

Tears streamed down Alex's face making it tough to see as he pulled the truck into a parking lot at the morgue. The trooper approached Alex's door. "I'll stay with the kids while you go in," he said. The trooper guided him to where Marge lay while the children sobbed softly in the beat-up pickup.

"We cleaned her up the best we could," the coroner told him. Alex nodded.

"Prepare yourself. She's not in good shape." Alex nodded again. As the man pulled the sheet back. Alex covered his mouth to keep from getting sick.

"NO!" he hollered as he ran out of the building and jumped behind the wheel of the truck.

"Is Momma really dead?" Bruce whimpered.

Alex was sweating profusely. He had a hard time catching his breath. "Yes, yes. She's gone." They all cried until their father quieted them. "Crying won't help us now, kids. We have to plan a funeral for Mom." And I must avenge her death, he thought.

"Try not to let the grief consume you. Mom wants us to be happy. We'll love her in our hearts," Alice stated.

"Poor Mom never got to see the goldfish we bought," Bruce said.

"She sees them from heaven," Alice said and squeezed his hand.

When they pulled into their driveway, Marge's parents stood holding each other on the front porch. Alex knew they would help with the arrangements and the children. He had to tend to other business. He loved his wife. They were a team. He felt wronged. He drove to the hospital and entered the emergency room. He asked to see Terry Foley, the man who stole his life. Alex could see him sitting up in bed with his head in his hands, but a trooper would not let him visit the patient.

"We'll be taking him to county soon. You can see him there," he was told.

"Right! And his rich daddy will have him out in a flash!" Alex screamed at the policeman. "And I'm left with no wife. No mother for my kids."

"I'm sorry," the officer said sympathetically.

Alex went home to his kids, held them and assured them he would take good care of them. They had their memories. He also told them about the man who hit their mother. Tammy could see the hate and hurt in his eyes as he spoke of the Foley man.

"Please don't do anything to him, Daddy. We need you," she pleaded.

"I know," he said and kissed the top of her head.

Terry Foley was out on bail before Marge was buried two days later. Alex knew the Foleys owned the local police and politicians and felt the man would never have to pay for his crime as long as it was left to them. Fayette County courts were well known for valuing men over women. He felt dazed and asked Marge's parents to stay with the kids a while after the post funeral luncheon. He packed the 357 Magnum in the waist of his black slacks. His nerves were on edge, throat dry, hands and legs shaking. Perspiration soaked his clothes. He drove by the Foley Estate and parked two blocks from their black-topped driveway where he had full view of their comings and goings. He knew the dope-head would have to go out and get his fix sooner or later.

Meanwhile Terry Foley fought with his father who refused to let him leave the mansion. "You killed a mother of three!" he screamed at his son.

"Send them a check!" Terry screamed back. He then punched his aging father, knocking him to the floor. He ran to the six-car garage and jumped into the BMW. His father slowly picked himself up and scurried to the door. "You'll pay for this. I won't help you again!" he yelled as his son sped away.

The BMW flew out into the road without slowing down. Alex started his truck. He waited for an 18-wheeler to pass. Terry swerved to miss the tractor trailer to no avail. Alex watched as the BMW spun underneath the trailer. He unloaded his pistol, called the authorities from a pay phone, and drove home to be with his family.

Ghostly

He was just floating through life, uninvolved with people and things. Working and eating and sleeping. Nothing seemed funny or important. It was not like being depressed. He did not really feel bad. He just did not feel at all. At the bar he acted like he listened when costumers talked to him. He nodded, let them know he was alive. Nothing more. Women followed him home. He would have a night and never pursue. His friends quit calling him because he was no fun.   Sometimes he would walk to the interstate and watch the cars go by. Life was going on. He could see, hear and smell it. He just could not feel it. When his paycheck was given to him he cashed it, paid the bills and bought food. Nothing special – canned pasta, bread, milk, prunes.

His tips were mediocre. They used to be twice as much at least. He did not care, barely noticed.

His youngest sister had twin boys. He never went to see them. They are now three years old.

He was not really aware of it. Not totally. The funk, I mean. Then late one night he closed the bar alone. As he cleared the cash register the sound of footsteps padded along the ceiling above in the attic. He went up there. The room was empty. Again, seconds later, he heard them clearer. Again, nothing there. He asked for the closing shift from then on. About twice a week the footsteps happened. Finally, he slept in the attic, lit a candle and waited.

After dozing, he was awakened by the rattling of dishes. He tiptoed down the ladder peeking around the corner into the dark kitchen. A foggy figure stood stacking bar glasses on the shelf above the double sink. An almost invisible thing. Ghostly, if you will.

"Who are you?" he asked a bit shaken.

"I live here," was the answer.

"Since when?"

35

"Since they shot me in '52."

"Well, why are you here now? I've never seen you in the four years I've worked here."

"You don't pay any attention. That's your problem," it said.

"Oh, really?"

"Yeah!" and it looked him in the eyes.

"Who are you then? Fifty two was a long time ago."

"Used to own this joint. Been watchin' things."

"Great. A ghost in residence."

"I'm more alive than you are," it sneered. "Never saw a more dead living human being than you."

No comment.

"You know I'm right."

"I guess."

"What are you waiting for? To be a spirit like me?"

"What do you propose? Christ, I'm talking to a ghost!"

"You don't talk to people. They're doin' you no good."

"So what is it? Seems you've got something in mind for me. You've been watching me."

"Someone needs to. You're wasting away."

"What's your name?"

"Vito Malansi."

"Who killed you?"

"Doesn't matter. We're talkin' about you. Why you walk around half dead."

"Do I?"

"God, can't you tell? You bore me and I'm dead! This used to be a fun bar. Not with you around."

"What is it you want?"

36

"Expression. Laughter."

"Maybe I'm in a slump."

"Slumps don't last this long."

"What then? What? I'm not suicidal like half my costumers. What do you want?"

"What do you want? That's the question. Just to get by and croak unnoticed? Don't you want to enjoy life?"

"It just all seems senseless. You live. You die. So what?"

"Maybe we should trade places. I wasn't done living when they shot me. You move into the attic. I'll tend the bar."

"Get real."

"This is as real as I get. I'm serious. It's boring up there. I want to have some fun."

"Don't you think anyone would notice? I can see through you for Christ's sake!"

"And I can see through you."

"Not in the same way. This is ludicrous."

"So is the way you just sort of float through life detached from everyone and never even smile. You don't deserve to breathe. I on the other hand would appreciate the chance to live."

"You're dead. It's too late for you."

"There has to be a way we can both get what we want. You want to die, obviously. I want to live. Let's talk about this over a drink. It's been a long time."

Everett made them both a scotch on the rocks. The good stuff. This was a bit of an occasion, he figured. "Here's to life," Vito said grinning.

"Very funny. You know, I thought you were a rat when I first heard you but your steps were too human-like, soft, but real."

"Putting out poison would have done you no good."

37

"I can see that. Do you think that drink will have any effect on you?"

"Yes. At least, I'm hoping. I used to love a scotch buzz."

"So, what am I going to do with you?"

"I think the question is what are we going to do about you."

"I'm waiting for your unearthly - forgive the pun - suggestions."

"You need gusto, boy. A new perspective. I can give you that."

"Yeah, how?"

"Let me in."

"In what?"

"In you. Take my spirit. Replace your own with mine."

Everett laughed for the first time in ages. It felt good.

"You can't be serious."

"Why not?"

"It's not possible."

"I thought it would not be possible to make you laugh again but you did. Feel better?"

"Yeah, sure."

"Take my hand. Let me melt into you. We can become one. Let Vito live again."

"Please don't touch me."

"You're afraid to touch the living and the dead. What's left?"

Everett woke in a sweat looking around the attic frantically. A large rat stared him in the eyes. He laughed. He went down the wobbly ladder laughing still. There was no one in the kitchen or the lounge area. He was alone with himself and his laughter. He walked outside in the morning sunlight and tore off his wet shirt. He jogged to the park and dove in the river feeling down right alive. Being touched by death will do that.

No Such Thing As Security

It was the largest house in town. Tracy Bennet supervised the building of it immediately after marrying Maxwell Bennet, computer genius. She decorated the sixteen spacious high-ceilinged rooms with a sharp eye for beauty. Rare antiques of brass, precious wood and china gave the small mansion a rich old-fashioned feeling. Tracy chose to marry the wealthy Mr. Bennet after her first marriage ended in divorce. She had decided to be practical. Love hurt too much. She sought security.

They moved to scenic Ruble Valley after the wedding so he could settle into writing a series of books. The only feature in the house that Maxwell had insisted on was his library and personal study. He had a huge wall length stone fire place installed. He told his wife it was pleasing to the eye and she agreed to the building of it insisting that he never bring firewood into their immaculate home.

Maxwell and Tracy were a handsome couple. Everyone said so. With her lush mane of coal black hair matching her eyes and his tall carriage and distinguished strong features. They were the talk of the tiny town since moving there eighteen months ago.

The day the workers put the finishing touches on his office Maxwell hired an assistant to help with his research. She left the job after two months. Since then he had worked with four different researchers. None had lasted longer than the first. Each time he told his wife the same thing, "She just wasn't working out." Tracy knew her husband was temperamental and understood the young people found him difficult to work for. The latest helper had stayed much longer than the others. Tracy was getting used to the studious Janet Kline when one day she did not show up at her usual time. When Tracy questioned her husband he shrugged his shoulders in his usual manner and told his wife that there was no reason that he knew of to explain her rudeness. They certainly had plenty of work to do, he assured her. Tracy took it upon herself to call Janet. Since the Bennet's arrival in Ruble Valley, Janet was the only person Tracy could call a friend. Janet was there to learn from a master unlike the previous employees who Tracy believed only took the job to be close to a rich handsome legend.

"Hello, Klines," the man answered.

"Yes, Mr. Kline, this is Mrs. Bennet. I was hoping to find Janet at home."

"Why she hasn't been home all weekend. Said she was going off on some business trip with your husband."

"Oh, she did. I had forgotten she was going along. Please have her call me when she gets in."

"Everything all right?"

"Just fine, goodbye."

Tracy sat the brass trimmed phone in its crook. She was proud to keep a secret for her new found friend and suspected she had snuck off with a young man although she had not mentioned anyone to her.

Janet had not showed up at work or home all week. The police questioned the Bennets unmercifully. After coming up with no motive for foul play the sheriff ruled her a runaway until some evidence was discovered to prove otherwise. Her vehicle was soon located south of town. No one was found in the area who had seen her.

Meanwhile, Maxwell had work to do. He had a deadline. His publishers wanted the first draft very soon. Then the police came calling, insisting that this was the second girl who disappeared recently. They had both worked for Maxwell. This knowledge frightened Tracy but her husband seemed unruffled by it.

The new assistant was a young man. He seemed efficient enough and life went on as usual. Tracy attended her biweekly antique shows and Maxwell's books were coming along on schedule. But Tracy could not shake the creepy feelings she got when thinking about the two girls. No trace of them yet. She had to know what really happened. Janet was not, in her opinion, runaway material. Maxwell seemed uninterested every time she brought up the subject at dinner.

"Young girls follow their hearts," he always reminded her. She knew this to be true from her own experiences but something seemed very wrong to her. She continued to question her controlled husband.

"Was there something going on with these girls? Is that why they all run out on such a cushy job when work is so difficult to find in this town?"

"Going on?"

"Yes. Did you have affairs with them?"

Maxwell looked at his wife. "Do you wish to stay married to me, security in tact?"

"I'd planned on it."

"Then quit this nagging. It's unlike you."

His aloof attitude turned Tracy's stomach. She always knew he was cold but she felt there was more to this. The missing girls seemed to haunt her thoughts making it difficult to concentrate on anything else. One afternoon when she was left alone in her home she wandered into Maxwell's study. It was the first time she had entered his sanctuary alone since the completion of the redecorating. It was obvious he had ordered the maid to stay out of there, too. Books and papers were strewn everywhere, even in the fireplace. The faint smell in the air was not the aroma of her husband's pipe tobacco. It had a burnt but rotting quality that both sickened and frightened her. She pulled the heavy curtains open letting the sun pour in. Something from the fireplace caught the sunlight and threw a glare across her dark eyes. She walked to the stone wall, bent down, and fished out a charred gold bracelet. It was Janet's, she knew. She dug farther only to find what seemed to be a small finger bone. Her heart jumped as she broke into a cold sweat, throat parched. She sat on the floor trying to decide her next step.

"Why?" she cried aloud.

Tracy's hands and legs trembled but she pulled herself to the phone. No wonder he made his helpers work in a separate office. Dialing the Sheriff's number, she wandered what she could possibly tell him. Maxwell had no reason to...

"Yes, Mrs. Bennet, I was just about to pay your husband a visit. I'll be right there."

The sheriff found Tracy in a state of shock. He lifted her from the floor and sat her in the desk chair forcing her to drink some cold water.

"Where is your husband?" I have some serious questions for him. I have reason to believe he has something to do with the disappearances. It seems your husband is no genius. He made his money stealing information from competitors. The girls I have interviewed who worked for him agree that he knows very little about the technology that he is writing about. He only compiles their findings. They were paid to keep quiet."

Tracy thrust a clenched fist toward the sheriff. I found these in the fireplace," she whispered as if saying it aloud would make it too real. "They belong to Janet Kline."

"My God! He burnt them!"

Just then the phone rang. The sheriff answered it. "Seems your husband drove into the canyon. The car caught fire when it hit. Tracy heard his words though they seemed far away. She would marry for love next time, she knew.

Makin' Change

"What's the special?"

"Up on the board," she told him with a tired sigh. "You've been sitting there for five minutes. Can't you see how busy I am?" her green eyes said in a flash.

"What's the soup of the day, then?" he inquired, enjoying getting under the skin of such a dark-haired beauty.

"Minestrone," she said flatly, tossing her thick mane over a slender shoulder.

"I'll take a small antipasto with Italian dressing on the side and a tall glass of ice water," the thin man said.

"Figures," she whispered to herself while hurrying back to the counter to retrieve drinks and desserts for tables one and six.

Bailey Nilliom was getting tired of the tiny spaghetti house she had been waiting tables in for the past year. Too many jerks, not enough tips to care. She yearned for a decent job, was tired of double shifts, and missed her son. She had moved back to the dingy little town to reunite with her mother and to give her son a sense of family. It was nice for a while but life had not been much fun lately. She yearned for a change. Friday nights at Cole Tavern was not her idea of a night on the town. She needed some allure and excitement in her life. The same old loud juke box, nasty pizza, and goofy guys really turned her off lately. She remembered feeling this way when she packed her blue jean bag and hitch hiked across the country when she was seventeen. She knew there was much more living to be done than swapping pasta and just scraping by. These thoughts crowded her mind lately making it difficult to concentrate on anything else.

"I said I wanted the dressing on the side, Miss. I demand a fresh antipasto!" the irritated man snapped as Bailey sat his order before him. He looked her in the eyes and mumbled, "Incompetent twit."

She moved closer to him. "What did you say?"

He held her gaze. If she had not been so irritated with his snobbish attitude she would have had a big laugh at the man's slicked-back hair. It seemed to glow above the brown square glasses.

"Incompetent twit!" he yelled at her for all the dining room to hear.

Bailey smiled at him with an ornery look in her eyes and calmly walked to the salad station. She brought his antipasto with Italian on the side toward him at a slow pace. He sipped his water feeling confident that he had straightened her out when she poured the oily dressing down the side of his beige tweed jacket.

"Italian on the side," she told him with a laugh.

He jumped to his feet with a screech that resembled a chicken's but she was out the door so quickly that no one had a chance to say a word to her. The other waitresses apologized to the soggy intellectual looking fellow when she brought him a damp cloth.

"Please send us your cleaning bill, Sir. I have no idea why she had to act so hatefully," she claimed.

"I want her name and address. She can take care of the coat. She can apologize," he told her.

The roads were slippery from the early spring snow storm that had taken place while she was working. Bailey had left her coat behind and was paying the consequences. The heater in her Volkswagen was worthless. She had forgotten to scrape the snow from the windshield in her rush to get out of there and the windshield wipers were having a difficult time removing the snow from her view. She looked behind her and thought she saw the man out on the sidewalk watching her pull away. Her windows were so icy she could not be sure it was him. Bailey laughed as she remembered the look on the man's face as she dressed him instead of his salad.

"He must have needed it. I know I did," she told

herself aloud. "Tonight I took a stand for abused waitresses across the globe." That was a step in the right direction, she was sure.

She rubbed the inside of the windshield trying to see the snow covered road. Her mind was jumbled with thoughts… Mom's going to be as mad as a cat; I'll go job hunting tomorrow; I'm moving on to better things. I'll find a job where I can get some respect and a nice paycheck every week; I need to play in the sun; this snow sucks. The thought of getting sun brightened her spirits as she turned into her mother's driveway. She dashed to the door - now nearly frozen. No one was home. With a sigh of relief she dropped into the easy chair that used to be her father's. Shivering, she covered herself with the afghan that lay over its back and closed her eyes.

"Hah!" she laughed out loud after a short nap. She threw the afghan to the floor. "Guess I showed that jerk. Won't be hasslin' hard workin' people anytime soon." She dropped to her knees in a fit of laughter until she realized her son was standing above her.

"Mom, are you OK? Did they send you home sick from work?"

"I'm OK, Hon. Help me up. Where ya been?"

"We went to the church fair I told you about," her mother said from behind the boy. "You should have gone if you weren't going to work, Bailey. Lots of nice people there. Alvin asked about you."

"Big thrill, Mom. I quit my job tonight, anyway."

"What? Use your head, girl. You have a son to sup-port."

"Don't worry. I'm going job hunting tomorrow. I've had it with waiting on people who think you are some brain-less slave. Me and Jake deserve better."

"What kind of job did you have in mind, Bailey? They need cleaning help at the church."

Bailey just could not bear to listen to the lecture she knew was coming so she left the room. "Clean the church? God!!" she screamed into her pillow as she dove onto her bed. "Doesn't anyone understand how I feel? Is it wrong to want more than what you have whether you have a super duper education or not? I just want to he happy," was her last thought as she dozed into a dreamy sleep.

The morning brought warm temperatures, and Bailey woke to sounds of snow melting and dripping from the roof. It splashed onto the ground from all sides of the house. Sun rays lightened and warmed the room. She rolled from her bed and opened the windows. It's a new day, she thought.

"Thought you were job hunting today. It's already 10:30," she heard her mother call to her from the doorway.

"After lunch is the time to call on the places I'm going."

"What places?"

"Every decent club and restaurant from here to Pittsburgh. I'm going to drive down Route 51 and stop at every p[lace that oozes money. Surely I can get a job where I don't have to work double shifts for a pittance. Wouldn't mind meeting some good men, too. The guys I know around here are not my type. Makes me think about becoming a nun."

"Oh, Bailey, the local fellas aren't that bad. Your father was one. May he rest in peace. You sure you don't want me to set up an interview for that cleaning job I mentioned?"

"Yes, I'm sure, Mom," she said with her best appreciative daughter look.

Bailey loved her mother, but they did not think alike. Not like she and Aunt Clare. Clare was a great listener, and Bailey felt a strong need to talk coming over her, so she picked up the phone and made an early lunch date. After a brief shower she dashed out the door enjoying the sunny morning. Her yellow VW was also happy about the warm

front. It started right up and never even stalled at the inter-
section.

"It is a beautiful day," she laughed, patting the dash-
board.

She found a parking place near the entrance of the
Howard Johnson's Restaurant. As she got out of the car she
noticed something in the back seat. It was the coat she had
left at work the night before. A note was rolled up and
sticking out of the side pocket.

"You must have been as cold as a pigeon in a snow
storm," the note said in type.

Clare came up behind her. "What's that you got, girl?"

"Just a note. No big deal." She smiled and hugged her
aunt. They went inside and settled into the corner booth.

"So what's the scoop, Bailey girl? I'm dying to know
what you're up to. Been kind of expectin' a change for you."

"That's just it. I quit my job last night. I dumped salad
dressing down some jerk's tweed jacket. He insisted he
wanted it on the side!"

"AHHH!" Clare cackled. "I bet he's not so demand-
ing from now on."

The ladies shared a big laugh over her departure from
the pasta house before they settled down and Bailey told
Clare her plan.

"I need a big change. Not really from the restaurant
business. I'm damn good at my job, but I'm dying to work
somewhere that I can make some money. Somewhere fancy
with people who know what a tip is. I don't mind working
hard, but, damn it, I'm tired of being a slave."

"What are you gonna do about it?"

"I need to borrow some clothes from you today so I
can cruise Route 51 and apply at the nicer places. I know the
perfect job awaits me. It has to."

"Let's finish our omlettes and go over to my place,
then. You pick out some outfits, and I'll drive you down

there. We'll have a good time shopping and celebrating after you hit the jackpot. You get what you grab in life, that's what I always say," Clare told her as she watched her red-haired reflection in the huge mirrored wall behind Bailey.

"Oh, thanks, Clare. Mom wants me to clean the church! I really appreciate your support."

The ladies left a nice tip for their waitress and left the restaurant arm in arm and all smiles and laughter. Bailey could not wait to rummage through her aunt's wardrobe. They met at her ivory covered house. Her second husband provided it in their divorce settlement, Bailey recalled. It had been years since she had the opportunity to play in the room Clare called her closet. She felt much like a child as they walked down the hallway that led to her eccentric auntie's wardrobe. She felt her life was about to change drastically.

Clare's walk-in closet-room was about the same size as her mother's living room. There were long shelves of sweaters, racks of dresses, skirts, slacks, and blouses and literally hundreds of pairs of shoes. Belts, scarves, and jewelry were strewn everywhere. Bailey was thrilled. She began by trying on several dresses and suits, and Clare found accessories to go with the outfits she chose. Many of the shoes were too tight, but she managed to find two pair that she could bear for short periods of time without screaming from the pain. One full wall was mirrored. Every girl's dream, she thought with a giggle.

"Think you'll make an impression in that red silk suit?" Clare asked her niece.

"You bet, but what kind? I think I'll take a few things along so I can change according to the place's style. Can we take your van?"

"Sure, Hon. I'd planned on it."

"This is my lucky day," Bailey sang as she dressed for the ride. She called her mom to say she'd be late and to please kiss Jake for her. She felt like a princess off to seek her fortune like in the fairy tales instead of a waitress looking for work, but she was not only job hunting. After spending her teens and early twenties partying and hitch hiking around the country, she was ready for a more comfortable way of living. She felt she had paid her dues by raising her son without a father and putting up with the creeps at the places she had worked. She was a good mother, and Jake was happy and healthy, but she wanted more for both of them. He deserved security, and Bailey herself needed a chance to grow into the woman she wanted to be... the woman she knew was buried within her just screaming to live. She had waited tables and tended bar from coast to coast and had become quite the professional at her trade. She knew she could thrive in the right place with the right people, and with Clare's help, she couldn't miss.

The ride did not seem long or tiring in the van with its cushy captain's chairs and stereo music. It was 2:30 p.m. when they arrived at the Blue Mirage Country Club. The place got rave reviews in the society papers and the food pages of the Sunday papers. The manager turned out to be a lady Bailey's age with similar working experiences. They got along well and She was told to call there Friday after lunch to find out of she could start part time on the weekends. The hourly pay was fair, and the tips were said to be top notch. She felt she may have a chance there but was determined to check out other places. She felt she was on a roll. They stopped at several more establishments, and one was hiring a hostess, but Bailey was not interested in a minimum wage job.

Clare spotted a large brick building that wore a distinguished sign bearing the name, The Pigeon Club." Let's pull in here. Wanna try it?"

"Sure. I wonder what the deal is about pigeons. Maybe they're bird watchers. I'll change into the gray flannel suit and go let them know they need my help," Bailey laughed, but she meant what she said. She pinned her hair up into a bun and donned her aunt's gray pumps.

"Knock 'em dead, lady," Clare encouraged her.

The door was locked but something drew her to knock on the large wooded mass that stood before her. She heard footsteps for a moment before the door opened.

"Hello. I'm Bailey Nilliom. I'd like to speak to the person in charge of hiring, please."

"Come in," the white-haired man told her.

She followed him up the steps and into his office which sat at the far side of a large sitting area. This was a sparsely furnished club with rich mahogany walls, floors and furniture. She sat opposite him, a huge wooden desk between them. She wondered how much oil soap it took to keep the place so shiny, but this was not the time for private jokes.

"Do you need any help here? I am seeking employment." she stated as she rose and shook his hand.

"I'm Mr. Williams. The agency was not supposed to send anyone until tomorrow."

"I am not from an agency. What sort of position is available?"

He explained that they needed a helper to serve brandy and wine to the wealthy and educated men who come there to talk, read and drink. She was intrigued by the feeling of the place. In this room important men make important decisions, she thought.

The man who interviewed her seemed ancient but youthful with his knowing eyes, strong body, dashing clothes, and thick, white hair. "In order to serve our fine wines and brandies you must become familiar with our cellar. We have an extensive collection. You would also be responsible for our library. Dust the books carefully, get them repaired when needed, keep them in their proper places, keep track of them.": Mr. Williams leaned his forearms on the desk and let them hold his weight as he brought his face closer to Bailey's.

"The person we need here must be discreet. We are a private men's club. We do nothing shady here, but much is said in the way of business and nothing can be discussed with family, friends, or anyone else."

Bailey's eyebrows grew together as she tensed her face into a questioning frown. "I assure you I can keep your secrets. I will give you references. As a professional bartender I've learned to keep much to myself. What a fine change it would be to serve civilized men," she heard herself saying. She felt brave and sophisticated in the rich surroundings. It was comfortable with its plush chairs, wooden floors and hundreds of books. She knew this was the job she wanted.

"We meet only two nights a week. Usually Tuesdays and Thursdays from 8 p.m. to 1 a.m. The pay is $300 a week plus gratuities if you prove to be who we need."

"When could I start?"

"You may stop here for a trial run on Thursday evening at eight sharp. That is tomorrow night. The door will be locked as it was today, but you shant go knocking. I shall entrust you with a key, but you must sign a form first. It states that you must use the key only for work hours. You are not to come here at any other time. It also states that we expect you to keep our trust. We can not afford to have leaks from our private conversations."

"I am intrigued. Where do I sign?" she was too excited to read the paper and wrote her name with a flourish.

"Please be prompt for work and dress in a casual but dressy manner - preppie, if you will. Come, I'll show you around."

What an interesting building it was with its rooms full of books and comfortable chairs, tables, and bars, she thought. Paintings of pigeons covered most every wall that had no book shelves. Everything was brass and wooden. The shining old floors seemed to have absorbed the years of secrets and thoughts of men. She wondered why he had hired a woman for their drink attendant/librarian. She had all but forgotten that Clare was waiting in the van when Mr. Williams showed her to the wine cellar. It was a study of fine old wines. Rows of bottles lined the walls. They were positioned by the year the wine was bottled for easy reference. A huge catalog sat on the butcher block table in the middle of the room.

"You will find the catalog very helpful until you get used to the arrangement here," he told her. "Our brandies are kept in the room behind that door." He pointed to the thick wooden door at the far end of the cellar. "Come. I'll show you."

The kind and fatherly ways of this man made Bailey feel at ease. She knew this was the change she needed but she could not quite put her finger on why. It was definitely not a bustling, exciting place. She liked and needed the feelings of strength and security the old building seemed to be giving her.

The brandy room was much like the wine cellar in the way it was set up. Bailey could hardly wait to sample these old delicate liquors.

They climbed the stairs to the main lobby. "If there are any questions you'd like to ask..."

"I think I've taken in enough for the first tour, but am I to serve food?" Bailey asked while wanting to scream from the ache of her poor feet.

"We have imported cheeses and caviar in the small kitchen behind those double doors if the men want a snack," he told her as he pointed to the large double doors just left of his office. "We don't come here to fill our bellies I assure you."

"Yes. Thank you for your time. I'll be here tomorrow at eight. Goodbye," she said as she shook her employer's hand. Bailey hurried down the loud wooden steps in dire need of kicking off her shoes, but she felt Mr. Williams watching her, so she suffered the pain of her size sevens squeezed into Clare's six and a halves. She threw the van's side door open and got rid of the shoes.

"How'd it go in there? It took you longer than…"

"I start tomorrow at eight. Let's celebrate," Bailey exploded as she changed into her shopping clothes.

"So, is this a bird watchers club or what?"

"No. It's a rich man's private club. They hired me to serve their fancy wines and brandies and to take care of their library of hard cover priceless books," she said with an air. They both laughed, but Bailey was thinking of the code of silence she had just signed her name to.

"I only have to work two nights a week for $300. plus tips. It's a little too perfect. You sure you didn't set this up with one of your beaus?"

"Don't blame me. Must be that charm of yours."

"Yea, no doubt," Bailey agreed. "You should see this place, though. Very manly and rich. I can't believe it. Must be dreamin' again."

"Let's go eat. I'm famished."

Bailey and Clare had a fine time shopping. They picked up several nice outfits for Bailey to wear to work. Wools, silks, and cottons. Bailey also bought a comfortable pair of shoes that matched everything. They ate raw oysters and Caesar salads and drank dark beer from frosted mugs. They drove home in a satisfied silence. Bailey's mind turned a thought per minute. She could hardly believe her good fortune.

"I got a job, Mom," she said at the breakfast table the next morning.

"So fast? Where?"

"It's about an hour's drive this side of Pittsburgh. A club along Route 51. Nice place. My luck is changing," she said confidently.

"Your old boss called yesterday. He's not happy with

you. Why would you do such a thing?"

"I couldn't help it. At least I didn't throw it in his snobbish face."

"You'll get the cleaning bill for his coat. They gave him your address."

"Great," she mumbled. But Bailey was not really listening to her mother, as usual. She rested and pampered herself all day while daydreaming about the sequence of events that took place the last couple of days and about her new job. If she had known that throwing salad dressing on some snob would have turned out so well, she would have done it sooner, she thought. She hoped this new place would open paths for her into a much nicer lifestyle. She hoped she was not about to serve brandy to a bunch of decrepit old men who smoked pipes between naps. She mentally began spending her paychecks.

The rush hour traffic had pretty well died down by the time Bailey had to leave for work. She felt grand in her warmly casual but studious outfit. She anticipated a quiet but interesting evening amongst men of power, cultured men who would speak to her with respect and ask her opinion about important worldly events. She knew she had better start reading the business page in the daily newspaper rather than first turning to the horoscopes and classified ads. She could not wait to read those wonderful old classic books on the shelves and to sip those wines and liquors. And reading! And more reading. It had been years since she had read anything in hardback. She missed the hours she had spent in the school libraries as a young girl and could not believe her luck in finding such a job so quickly and with no written resume! The timing seemed uncanny, but she just laughed it off to her Irish luck that was finally unveiling itself.

She arrived twenty minutes early to acquaint herself with her surroundings. The huge wooden door opened with a creak that she did not remember from the day before. Her very loud footsteps on the bare wooden stairway would announce her presence to anyone who was in the club. No one came to greet her when she called out so she went to the office. She knocked and waited. The place seemed to be deserted. She knocked again and noticed an echo but no answer. She tried the door knob. It was locked.

"Damn!" she whispered. "Where are the men?"

She walked to the center of the main room and studied the bookshelves. She chose a book of short stories by Hawthorne and sat down to read "The Fox." It was 8:10 p.m. when she checked her watch again.

"Eight o'clock sharp, my butt," she muttered.

An odd feeling stirred in her as she approached the office again. No one answered her very loud knock. She turned the handle, and the door opened slightly. She stepped back to think, positive the door had been locked when she tried it earlier. With a soft push the door opened wide enough to see that no one was in the room.

"What the hell?" she whispered to herself as she walked up to the desk.

An antipasto sat in the center of the desk. Beside it lay a beige tweed jacket with an oil stain on its side. No one but the echo answered her cry. She searched for a note to no avail. A leather bound dictionary lay open beckoning her to read the highlighted text.

Pigeon - a family of birds with small heads. Slang, one easily swindled.

Blood rushed to her head. Her breath became short. Her limbs were weak and shaky. She heard footsteps coming from the room she was told was the kitchen. He came through a door that Bailey had assumed was a closet. She was leaning on a chair, bewildered. The tall slick-haired man smiled at Bailey.

"I'm glad you'll not be serving meals."

The Town Pest

She annoyed everyone who knew her, except Grace. Her parents had warned her many times. "Mind your own business. That big mouth of yours will get you in trouble one day." But she could not seem to keep herself from pushing her opinions on all those who tried to get ahead.

Some said it was jealousy, but she had more than most. Patty herself would tell you, if someone had not drowned her last night, that it was for the betterment of the community. No one believed that crap.

Out of one hundred or so people who lived in Laurel Falls, Pennsylvania, probably 90 percent of them had a motive to kill Patty Franks. They all knew she was a poor swimmer and scared to death of the water since her sister went over Laurel Falls when they were young. She had gossiped about everyone at one time or another.

Some say she wanted to die - that losing her sister in front of her eyes snapped something in her mind long ago - That being the town pest was her way of paying life back for being so cruel.

Now she was gone, and Sheriff Ed Torence stood in his ex-lover's living room talking to a rookie state cop.

"Who do you think would do it, Sheriff? You know everyone. Let's rap this up quick as we can," the officer said.

Recca Mitchum was the mayor at this time. She and her uncle, the new sheriff, were not happy. They kept things pretty well under control in the village and did not feel they needed outside help. Did not want it.

"I'll keep you posted as my investigation progresses. No sense in your worrying your mind over this," Sheriff Torrence told the officer.

"Do you two know something I should know?"

"No doubt, but not about this," the sheriff laughed.

"Sir, no disrespect intended, but this is a serious

matter. A woman's life was taken..."

"Look, Son, no one will get away with murder, but this is my problem, although I appreciate your concern."

Recca winked at the nervous officer as he walked out the door. "Uncle Ed, I know you are hurting, but we have to co-operate with the States."

"Glad to see you're on my side."

"I am always on your side. Come on. I know you loved her in your own way but we have to keep our heads. We knew this would happen sooner or later."

"You're right. OK. Are you saying you think she jumped or someone helped her?"

Recca threw her dark hair back and sighed, "I've been watching for a flinch of guilt. Someone who's avoiding me. Just that look that says, 'Hell, yes, I did it and I'm not sorry.' But I haven't seen it. What about you?"

"No. Not yet. Seems to me we should go to the wake and keep our eyes and ears open."

After the funeral Patty's family held an Irish wake for their daughter. They rented the upstairs of the Deer Run Tavern, and the place was packed when the Sheriff arrived. He paid his respects to her parents and made his way to the bar. He no sooner got a glass of ginger ale served to him when Grace Wilhelm, Patty's only friend, approached him with hate in her eyes.

"I hope you are happy. You finally got rid of her," she accused.

"Grace, I'm as sorry about his as you are."

"Is that right? Then why are you standin' here like a bump on a log and not out arresting her killer?"

A hand lay firmly on her shoulder - turning her completely around. Recca had grown up with Grace. They were next door neighbors for a score of years, and although they were not actually friends, Grace did respect the mayor and allowed her to guide her away to the restroom to regroup.

"I have no friends left!" Grace wailed, crying hysterically. "You have to find out who did this!"

"Don't worry. I have no intention of letting this go. You'll have to trust me on that."

"I'm so alone now," she stared at the mayor.

"If you need to talk, I'm always available."

"Thanks, Recca. What really gets me is everyone seems so smug. Like they finally got their fondest wish. No one here really cared about her."

"I can't bring her back for you, but if you settle down and let Ed do his job, we will find the murderer and punish accordingly."

As they joined the party, Recca made her way through the crowd to her uncle.

"Great timing. I owe you one."

"She knows you, Uncle Ed. She's just upset and mad as hell. Thinks everyone's happy Patty's dead."

"Seems like a lot of people are," he nodded toward the pool table.

Gene Waber and his little brother, Wade, were arguing. "OK, smart ass. You think you know it all. We'll take a vote."

They passed the cocktail napkins around to about 14 people and told them to write down the three most likely murder suspects.

"We'll just see who everyone else thinks it is," Gene told his little brother, who thought he really knew.

Spectators had gathered and tensions were running high. Artie Ramps took his wife and children out of there shaking his head, but Recca and the sheriff watched.

When they tallied the votes, Gene let Wade read them off.

"Looks like Tom McGraft got most of the votes followed by Marie Standish and our own Sheriff. Gee folks.

That's not very nice. What's he gonna do, arrest himself? I still think you're all wrong."

"Then tell us who it is," Sheriff Torence stepped up. "Thanks for the confidence, folks." He eyed the crowd with contempt.

"Sheriff, didn't see you there."

"Obviously. And you didn't answer my question. What makes you think you know? Did you see something?"

"No. Just shootin' off my big mouth. You know me."

"Yeah. Think it's time you people went home. This is a serious investigation. Unless you have some real evidence to offer, I better not hear of this ignorance again."

Tom McGraft came up to the sheriff as everyone filed out of the tavern. "It wasn't me," he mumbled. "I know I felt like killing her, but I don't have it in me." he pleaded.

"Never thought you did, Tom. That injunction on your place can't hold for long. Forgive her and go about your business."

Thanks, Sheriff."

The inside of Patty's home was seemingly undisturbed. The deck had a chair upset and a few plants turned over. That was it. But the sheriff went through her things again just in case there was something his grief made him unaware of. She kept meticulous files on all her law-suits, but he knew who she was pissing off, and none of them, in his opinion, could have done it. Her place was secluded. It would be easy enough to make noise outside and grab her when she came to shoo away what she thought was a cat. Whoever it was did just that, he was almost sure. She was then forced to the river and held under. Guilt filled him. If he had married her like she wanted, this would not have happened. And he felt someone was laughing at him. Thought he was getting old. Too old to figure out who killed a lady he had cared for. The blatant disrespect ate at him. And then he found a ring he had never seen before. It was still in its box, obviously new. A ruby.

A pang of jealousy went through him, and he laughed at himself. He will miss her attentions. It was her intentions that made him shy away.

He took the ring to Grace, who knew nothing about it, so he headed to the area jewelry stores.

"May I have a word with you in private?" he asked the elderly lady behind the counter filled with gold and diamonds.

"Come this way, officer," she said, walking to the rear of the store where her desk sat.

"I need to know who purchased this ring." He laid the ruby ring before her.

"I believe this is the ring I just adjusted to fit that lady who was killed."

"Patty Franks."

"Yes. I recognized her when her picture was in the paper. I believe it was a gift to her."

She checked her files and came back with a yellow receipt in her small, wrinkled hand.

"We have to talk," he said, pulling Recca away from her dinner. He explained the story as they drove to Artie Ramp's house to question him.

Artie and his family were sitting at the dinner table when they arrived. He bolted for the back door, and Recca ran after him. She was faster than him, and she dove, tackling him by the legs. The sheriff stood over them holding the gun on Artie. The youngsters cried, and Sophie Ramps had that knowing look wives get when their worst fears come true.

"Why, Artie? How could you do it?" the sheriff asked him.

"She just wouldn't shut up!" he kept repeating.

Everyone understood, even the children.

Cautious Encounter

When Lacy stepped into the grocery store line, she noticed the handsome older man in front of her. No ring on either hand. It was the second thing she looked for. The first was a gentleness in the eyes.

"Any coupons?" asked the cashier.

"No. Not today," she said, embarrassed to have been day dreaming. Her mom always said she did not pay attention.

With all the nuts and diseases out there, Lacy was careful about her romantic relationships. So careful she had just spent six months alone. Lacy Marrow was cautiously eager for love. Her friends were great company, but she yearned to be held, touched, and appreciated.

The salt and pepper haired man turned to her, putting his green stamps in her hands, smiling. He just as quickly turned back to his shopping cart and proceeded to steer it through the automatic doors and into the parking lot. Lacy hurriedly paid for her things and dashed to the exit.

She caught a glimpse of the dark-eyed fellow as he got behind the wheel of his new black Volvo and pulled the door closed.

She did not have far to run but got somewhat carried away pushing the buggy at a high rate of speed. She laughed to herself and slowed to a mere jog, passing the Volvo with her best nonchalant gait. (As cool as one can get when they're out of breath, heart pounding).

He wound his window down and slowly moved his vehicle close to hers. Lacy had just opened the hatch of her old Chevrolet when he spoke.

"Excuse me, Miss."

Lacy tried not to smile too widely. "May I help you?" she asked.

"I hope so. I don't mean to be rude or pushy, but I

noticed you in the store."

Lacy waved the stamps at him.

"Could we meet for lunch somewhere if you're not busy?

"Do you have a name?" she asked, approaching his car.

"Morgan. Morgan Davis."

She introduced herself, and they shook hands. She was enjoying the time to flirt.

"I can get us a table at the cafe down by the river. It's on the corner."

"Yes, I know it. I could meet you in an hour."

"I'll be waiting," he said and pulled away from her with a wink.

Lacy watched him leave the parking lot and head south toward the river. She got herself home in a bit of a panic. The excitement really got to her once inside the apartment, and she burst into a loud squeal, jumping around and tossing pillows in the air. She decided not to change clothes since he would surely take note of it.

A wasp buzzed at her sliding glass door. She slid it open, let it out, and stepped onto the patio. It was a sunny day. Her many plants thrived and gave her small third floor deck a greenhouse effect. Lacy took her golden hair from the clip and leaned her head back to shake it full. After cleaning up and giving her hair a good brushing, so she grabbed her keys and headed to lunch with a stranger. Her friend had met a nice man in the grocery store. Maybe this was her lucky day.

After the most delightful lunch, Lacy caught four green lights in a row and was home in record time. She was happy but a little drowsy, so she relaxed on the redwood lounge on the patio. The sun was moving around the yellow brick building she had called home the last three years. Lacy dozed in the early evening breeze.

Her dreams took her to Morgan's boat. They were

fishing. She even caught a small one. Their day was filled with warm caresses, sexy looks, and heated necking sessions. After dinner, Morgan became abusive in his language and manner. He had by then consumed a full bottle of gin. He grabbed her and pulled her against him, kissing her more with his teeth than his lips. Lacy pushed him away, but he got her by the arm.

"Lacy," he said gently shaking her shoulder.

She jumped from the chair and grabbed the wasp spray that sat next to her chair. She was still very shaky from her dream.

"Don't do it. The door was unlocked. I thought you might like to take a ride with me. I'm sorry I startled you."

She sat down and shook her head to get rid of the cobwebs.

"I knocked, but you didn't answer. The door was open. Were you dreaming? You seemed so alarmed - frightened."

"You almost got sprayed."

"Next time I'll throw stones at your windows," he promised, putting his arm around her and pulling her to her feet. "I hope I am not an unwanted pest."

"I hope not, too," she smiled.

Poor Harry

"Harry hunted there a couple times a year," Alice Nore told the officers.

"Yes, Ma'am. If I have anymore questions I'll call. Sorry to have bothered you."

Alice closed the door and leaned her round physique solidly against it. He is dead. No more Harry. No more cooking, no more snoring, no more living with a drunken bum who fancied himself the great white hunter. The house was so quiet she could hear her breath, until Lori barked sharply from the sun porch. Alice went to her companion.

"It's just you and me now, Babe," she told her, petting soft white curls.

Alice sang as she donned her black silk tunic and set off for the funeral home where her husband was being shown. She had given the mortician Harry's only suit. She hoped it had still fit him. Friends and relatives filled the parlor to pay their respects. The room overflowed with flowers from hunting buddies all over the world. Talk of the accident soon filled the room.

It was general knowledge that Harry was a pro with a rifle. It was unthinkable that he should die this way. Alice did not agree. She had warned him often enough. She knew he slept with his favorite gun and was not surprised he should die by it.

They buried him on a foggy morning. There was a steady drizzle during the outdoor service. Alice was anxious to be getting home. Lori was alone. They had a new life to live. Alice had every intention of forgetting about her husband as soon as she could. She had loved him once, but years of his drinking and carousing had killed that love long ago. Since his death, she had not shed one tear, and none of her close friends blamed her.

Alice was always happy to see Harry going off on

one of his hunting trips. It got him out of the house for weeks at a time. He used to come home drunk and drag her out of bed to fight. He often hit her until one night she crowned him with a cast iron skillet.

"You hurt me," he whined when he came to.

"You leave me alone from now on," she warned.

That was almost a decade ago. Harry found someone else to fight with and sleep with in his drunken stupors. Alice was thrilled. She did not believe in divorce but was happy to be relieved of her wifely duties.

Before leaving for this last hunting trip, Harry said to his wife, "I'm goin' alone. Need to be by myself. I'm tired of bein' put down by women. I'm not that bad, am I, Alice?"

"Fightin' with her, huh?"

"Hummph!" he sounded, giving her a sneer.

Alice never mentioned her before but knew who she was and wondered why she wasted her time with Harry.

Twenty-six years they had been married. Alice worked. She owned the house. She had her savings and her dreams. She did not miss Harry. Going through his things now, she felt detached. They could have belonged to a stranger. She felt no grief - only a tremendous sense of freedom. She boxed everything up and sent it to the church center. She redecorated the house to erase any trace of his having lived there for a quarter of a century. She took great pleasure in destroying his favorite easy chair. She could not count the times he had passed out on it, snoring like a hyena. She had rooms painted, carpets replaced, and new furniture moved in. Alice looked around her new abode. She felt pleased and treated herself to an espresso while curling up on the new plush sofa with Lori. "Life is good," she sighed.

Alice answered the door bell on the third ring. She was standing there looking distraught and haggard. Her eyes and nose were puffed and red from crying.

"Mrs. Nore, I was a friend of Harry's," she said,

visibly shaken.

"I know who you are. Come in," Alice said.

They sat across from each other in new overstuffed chairs.

"You know?" she asked, not believing what she heard.

"Of course," Alice assured her.

"I killed him," she said quietly. "He left me, so I..."

"What?"

"It's true."

"No!" Alice said. "What do you mean?"

"I followed him to the cabin and shot him in his sleep."

"What?!" Alice was shocked.

"I shot him."

Alice stood and paced the floor. She loved the feeling of the thick carpet between her toes and had to stifle a laugh. "You're serious, aren't you?"

"Yes. I've been so scared and nervous I had to tell someone. Go ahead and call the police."

"The police? Oh no. No police," Alice told her, sitting across from her again.

"Why not?"

"I'm not going to have you put in jail for giving me the freedom I've dreamed of for years. I'm glad he's dead," Alice said.

"He was your husband! I loved him, but he left me to come back to you!"

"He never left me. I wish he had."

"You know what I mean."

"He was upset when he left for the cabin, but he got no sympathy from me."

"I see. You hated him."

"He disgusted me, yes."

"Now what?"

71

"Go home," Alice told her. "Try to forget. No one will know this from me. Go to confession and relieve your conscience."

She walked slowly to the door, gave Alice a long look, and went to her car. Alice leaned against the closed door and let out the belly laugh she had held in for too long.

"Poor Harry," she said. "I like his taste in women."

Late Bloomin'

Nancy Shaw was always kind of a loner. Her mousey brown hair had been cut into a "pixie" for twenty-four years. Lucky for her, the first year of her life she was bald. She slept twelve hours every night and studied her spare time away to try and escape her loneliness. Being shy and homely left her with no friends, and her folks were no help. Their old-fashioned ways kept her in a shell.

After graduating from a local college, Nancy took a job at a National Park in Southern Florida. This was a big step for her. She had never been out of New York. She would be working in the large camping areas in the park, checking people in and out, dolling out information, and helping to see that visitors had an enjoyable stay. There would be no town for sixty miles. Only swamp, alligators, snakes and flamingos.

For the first time in her boring life she was going off without her overprotective mother. "Butterflies" filled her stomach as she imagined herself living in a hut in the tropics so far away.

She decided to take a train and see the country. This worked out well to Miami, and then she had to take a cab the whole way to Everglades National Park. She was a long way from home.

Most of her coworkers had that slow southern drawl she had heard about. At times it was difficult to understand what they were saying, but it was getting easier.

The winter season brought more people to the park than she thought possible. Camping was free. So was fishing if you had your own boat. Otherwise you could rent one at the marina or take a guided trip. Nancy had no desire to catch fish. She loved the pink flamingos and often took the walking paths through the woods in hopes of coming upon a flock or perhaps a small deer.

During the first few months Nancy became an efficient employee, but she was still lonely. She got along with her coworkers but had not made many real friends. Her daily walks became a ritual, and her hair grew for lack of a barber. She liked the idea of improving on the hair cut.

"Is there someone who does hair around here?" she got up the nerve to ask a cafeteria worker one day as she went through the line gathering her breakfast.

"I do me own," the Cuban lady said.

Nancy excused herself and took the table along the wall. She pulled a small mirror from her purse and studied her image, keeping her back to the other diners. She had never tried styling her hair and was unsure where to start.

"Mind if I sit?" the short, plump man of thirty asked her. "There's no where else."

"Go ahead," she said, signaling with one hand while putting the mirror away with the other.

"I'm Marvin Schenlick." He offered his hand.

"Nancy Shaw," she blurted, shaking his sweaty paw.

"Another hot one today," he said, his mouth full of pastry.

"Yes." She was not comfortable with small talk and wanted to run out of there.

"Don't you want your doughnut?" he asked, licking his full lips.

"No. Go ahead." Nancy watched the balding man swallow the pastry whole while slugging a full glass of chocolate milk. She smiled at the funny man now almost enjoying his piggish manners.

"You a ranger?" he asked.

"I work in the campgrounds."

"Busy, I bet."

"Yes."

"I bet," he repeated, studying her with his narrow grey eyes. "Are you seeing anyone?"

74

Nancy was unsure of what he meant but guessed her wanted to know if she had a boyfriend. She blushed. "Not really."

"I'm here with relatives I can't stand for another week. Could we have dinner later?"

"I guess it would be all right," she said, accepting her first date. Twenty-four and never been kissed. She almost laughed at herself and at the funny but serious man facing her.

"Let's meet in the dining room at seven then."

"Fine," she agreed, getting up to go put in her daily shift.

They nodded to each other, and he sat back down to finish his pancakes.

Outside the building in the bright sun, Nancy walked briskly, giggling all the while at the feelings stirring inside her. No man had ever so much as looked her way, but now she was going on her first date. He was no Prince Charming, she knew. But he looked at her and talked to her and ate her doughnut. She raced for the campground, wishing for time to move quickly to the evening.

She sat in front of the large mirrored vanity in her cottage, scissors in hand. She had bought some styling gel and a hair dryer at the marina store and now read the magazine again.

"I should be able to look like that!" she told herself aloud, planning to follow the instructions about no-fuss hair styles.

She gave herself a trim and washed her hair. She applied the gel and blew it dry using a round brush. She could not believe that she looked soft and feminine for the first time in her life. Choosing an outfit from her bland wardrobe made her promise herself a shopping trip soon. It was difficult with no car, but she was saving up for one.

Wishing she had not arrived so early, she sat watching

for him from the corner booth. Marvin showed up just as she had decided to take to the lady's room.

"Going to stand me up, were you?"

"Just thought I'd powder my nose." She had heard the excuse on television and could not believe it when she said it.

"You need no makeup with that skin of yours," he said.

The compliment made her blush even though it was given so matter-of-factly. She enjoyed the heated sensation in her face. Such feelings had not been a part of her past. She did not care that the man slugged down three martinis before she finished her first cola. She was on a date.

Marvin ordered for both of them without inquiring as to her preference while she smiled politely. He ate his four-course meal, two of her courses, burped, and ordered more gin with their cheesecake.

"I'd like to see you again," he stated with no emotion.

"That would be nice," she told him.

After he had several more drinks he paid the check and asked her to leave the tip. This took her back a step, but she decided it was little to ask after the expensive meal.

He drove Nancy to her cottage and turned the car off, taking her hand roughly and placing it between his legs. She pulled away and got out of the car.

"What's wrong with you?" he snorted. "I thought you liked me."

"So did I. I have to wash my hair," she said and quickly sprinted to the door.

He peeled out of the gravel parking lot, leaving a cloud of dust. Nancy shook the angry, insulted feelings that were developing and took a long walk to clear her mind. She had no intentions of washing away her new do. It was just another one of those excuses that women always used. She had waited so long to say them to a man that they slipped from her automatically tonight.

The next morning she went through the cafeteria line for breakfast as always. The Cuban lady smiled at her and shook her head up and down with approval.

"Good morning," she said and went to her favorite table.

She was spreading jelly on her English muffin when she heard a commotion across the room. It was Marvin. He was taking a cinnamon roll from a lady twice his size.

"I'm eating that!" she heard her yell while slapping his sticky hand.

"Sorry, Ma," was all she heard Marvin say.

A lanky dark-haired nerd type gave her an interested look from the corner booth where he sat alone. Nancy smiled at the man in the brown square glasses, saying a prayer so that he would not come by and ask for her doughnut.

Nobody's Child

She named the boy Lenny. He was a basically healthy infant but had several accidents and illnesses through his first years of life. These were caused mainly by neglect. Lenny was more often alone than not. He spent many nights sleeping in his mother's car outside one dive bar or another. Many times Lenny would wake up in the back seat and rub the sleep from his eyes only to go in and hang around until his mother was ready to go home. Everyone said, "He's sooo cute," and they gave him drinks of beer and taught him their philosophies of life and love.

After he started school, his mother tried to cut down on her drinking and carousing. They would spend only two or three nights a week out on the town rather than the usual five or six. She gave herself a pat on the back for the sacrifices she was making for the good of her child. This lasted for almost a year at which point his mother announced to him:

"Lenny, you are six years old now. Gettin' to be a big kid. Big enough to stay at home an' watch TV while I go out for a while. My kid's growin' up," she beamed at her dark-eyed child.

"By myself, Mama?"

"Don't worry, Hon. You'll be OK. Keep the door locked and I'll be home before you fall asleep. Don't stay up waitin' on me. You gotta rest for school tomorrow." She kissed his forehead and rushed out the door.

Lenny made himself a jelly sandwich and turned on the TV. He plopped down on the old lumpy couch and woke for a short second when his mother carried him to bed. It was almost daylight, he knew.

For years he spent many nights this way. He rarely did his school work, but no one seemed to notice. He passed in school by the skin of his teeth.

His mother rarely brought her dates home. That was not good for her boy, she often told them. Once in a while she came home a day or two later. This was one of those times. She left almost two days ago to celebrate her son's tenth birthday. Lenny wanted to have a party of his own. He had never run the streets. Momma did not allow it. She did not take him with her anymore, either. He had the ten dollar bill she had given him for his birthday before she left. He showered and pulled on his cleanest jeans and shirt. He styled his hair with his mother's gel and grabbed his denim jacket. Looking good, he smiled at himself in the mirror before walking out the door. Lenny patted his front pocket to make sure his money had not escaped and stuck his thumb out to catch a ride.

An old Plymouth station wagon pulled up next to him, smoke rolling out of the exhaust pipe.

"Get in, kid," the burly cigar-puffing man said.

Lenny got in.

"Where do you live? I'll take you home," the man eyed him. "You shouldn't be out here hitchhikin'."

The large man's concern for him tugged at Lenny's heart. "I'm tired of sittin' home alone. I been tired of it," Lenny insisted.

"My name's Gene. Are you hungry?"

"Yeah. I was lookin' to go get a burger to celebrate my birthday. Can you take me to a diner?"

"Your birthday? How old are you, son?" Gene pulled the old clunker back on the road and headed toward town. "You could go home with me. I know my Thelma baked a chocolate cake this morning. Bet we could hunt up some candles."

Lenny stared at the man. "Are you serious? You're not some weirdo, are ya?"

"I'm harmless. I promise. But you're real lucky some nut didn't pick you up."

"I never hitchhiked before. I live on Tenth Street. If it's not too far away I wouldn't mind a piece of cake."

"You can go home anytime you want. Just say so."

"OK, it's a deal," Lenny agreed, feeling better just being with someone for a while. His school friends played ball but their parents had to drive them back and forth to practice and games. His mother sold her car a while back to cover rent. He wasn't encouraged to do anything.

Lenny could see they were heading out of town.

"You sure you have a Thelma?" he asked, wandering if he had made a mistake in trusting the big man called Gene.

"Almost home. You'll love Thelma. You'll see." Gene smiled at the boy and mussed up his soft brown hair. Lenny did not mind at all.

Gene pulled the wagon into a gravel parking place in front of a big old wooden farmhouse. The lawn was crowded with bikes, a swing set, a sand box, a see saw, bats and balls.

"Wow!" Lenny gasped.

They walked in through the back door and entered a kitchen bustling with kids form toddlers to teens. Seven in all, Lenny counted.

"Thelma, honey, this is Lenny. It's his birthday. I invited him to join us."

"Glad to meet you, Lenny," the sweet looking lady said. "Take a seat and dig in. The kids have just finished eating." She handed him a plate, silverware and a glass of milk. Lenny took a seat on the bench. He had never seen a picnic table indoors before. Most of the kids introduced themselves to him and made him feel welcome and comfortable. Thelma put candles on the cake while the oldest boy cleared the table. Lisa was about his age, he figured. She brought the layer cake, placing it in front of him. Gene lit the candles, which his wife had shaped into a number ten.

"Make a wish," Lisa said giggling.

Lenny closed his eyes and wished he could have a

family like Gene's. He blew the candles out in one big gust. A boy of about four snatched the candles out of the cake and licked the icing from them. Lenny could barely control the elation he felt sitting in this homey kitchen next to a girl he already liked a lot.

"Ice cream, Lenny?" Gene asked as he dipped scoops for the clan.

"Sure," he said shyly. He gobbled his birthday cake and thanked Thelma for the second piece she quickly placed in front of him.

"Can you stay and play Monopoly, Lenny?" Lisa asked.

"Sure," was all he could say.

They played for a couple hours when Lenny realized he should get home. Gene could see the indecision in his face and saved him the trouble of speaking up.

"You look tired, Lenny. Better get you home before your folks call the National Guard."

All the kids said their goodbyes. Thelma kissed his cheek, and Lisa grabbed his hand and put a piece of paper in it. He shoved it in his pocket and felt the ten dollars he never spent.

When Gene pulled the car up to the curb in front of Lenny's apartment building he wished the boy a happy birthday.

"Thanks. It was really great," Lenny said while opening the car door.

"Our last name is Troutman. We're in the book. Call anytime, kid. I mean it."

"I will," he promised and pushed the rusty door closed.

"Hey!" Gene hollered. "No more hitchhikin, OK?"

"OK," Lenny yelled, waving.

As he climbed the stairs Lenny took the paper from his pocket.

"Call me tomorrow. 461-9204, Lisa," it said.

Lenny kissed the note knowing he wasn't alone anymore.

The Killjoy Cookie

After being there so many times in her life, sitting at her mother's kitchen table now brought memories of fun and laughter over lemonade and cookies with the neighbor kids. Mom always made the best cookies. Then at her pre-teen parties, crying over boys, Mom always just seemed to be there. A permanent unquestionable figure, she assumed. Her caretaker. But where was she now?

Her father was frantic when he called. She could tell he was trying to be calm. "Have you seen your mother?" he asked. "She's hours late from that play she had to go to. I looked everywhere."

She did not know what to say.

"I checked the hospitals," he added.

"I'll be right over," she assured him and hung up the phone.

It was 4 a.m. Her mind slowly began to function and conjure up ideas of what may have happened to her mother. "I hope she was carrying her mace," she thought. "Maybe she'll show up before I do." The forty mile drive gave her a chance to think. She knew her mother to be an organized considerate lady who would never go off somewhere without letting her husband know. Millie Frey was sure of this.

She sat at the kitchen table with her father. An eerie feeling enveloped her as she agreed to go to the theater with him.

"I'll drive," was all she could say.

They rose and walked to the car with no other words. She did not want to burden her father with negative thoughts.

It was almost 6 a.m. when they arrived at the theater. There were no lights on in the office building. They knocked continuously anyway. No one answered.

"Where the hell could she be?" her father cried. "She

begged me to go to the show with her, but I refused. You know how I hate those things. And now she's..."

"We'll find her, Dad. Don't worry yet. Let's check the all-night diner. Maybe she went there with friends for coffee."

"She would have called."

As Millie glanced back at the building she noticed a shadow watching them from a window. She ran and beat on it fiercely, yelling, "I know you're in there. Please come to the door. It is very important."

Footsteps walked away from her. She ran back to her father who sat wearily on the front steps with his head in his hands. They heard the click of the lock and watched the door open slightly.

"What do you want?" a man asked.

"We're looking for someone who attended the show tonight," she blurted as she showed him the snapshot of her mother with her blue ribbon from the church cookie contest. "Have you seen her?"

"I'm the janitor, Ma'am. There is no one else here. Sorry."

"Thanks anyway," she said.

"I don't trust him. Let's ask him some more questions," her father demanded.

"He doesn't know anything, Dad. Let's check out the diner."

They showed the photograph around to no avail. "I'm going to call the police," Millie told him.

"Let's go home and call."

Millie fought back panic as she followed him into the kitchen. If she had not seen the terror in his eyes she would have never believed the truth. Her mother sat at the kitchen table bruised, swelled, alive, wet and filthy. She was exhausted.

"Mom!!" I screamed.

"Hi," she whispered, staring hatefully at her husband.

"What happened?" I asked in tears holding her torn hands.

"Ask your father."

"Daddy?"

He stumbled over a chair and ran out the door.

"Daddy?!!" she screamed after him.

"I better get you a doctor. What the hell's going on?"

"I'll be all right."

"Mom, tell me what happened."

"Your dad beat me up last night real bad because I won't give him a divorce. He has a girlfriend. He must have thought he killed me, because he dumped me in Thompson's Pond."

"Dad? You gonna let him get away with this?"

"No, honey. Check the cookie jar."

"I'm not hungry."

"Check it."

"It's empty."

"Help me pack."

"I guess I won't ask what kind of cookie I missed."

"Good idea."

More Titles by Marci McGuinness

Gone to Ohiopyle (Fall 2009)

Hauntings of Pittsburgh & the Laurel Highlands (Fall 2009)

Butch's Smack Your Lipss BBQ Cookbook (Spring 2009)

How to be a Working Author/Writer (2005; 2nd Edition, Fall 2008)

Chesapeake Bay Blue Crabs (2004)

In it to Win It (2001)

The Explorer's Guide to the Youghiogheny River, Ohiopyle and SW PA Villages (2000)

Along the Baltimore & Ohio Railroad, from Cumberland to Uniontown (1998)

Stone House Legends & Lore (1998)

Yesteryear at the Uniontown Speedway (1996)

Official Program U.S.A. Speedway, 1916 Reprint (1996)

Yesteryear in Ohiopyle - The Movie

Yesteryear in Smithfield (1996)

Yesteryear in Masontown (1994)

Yesteryear in Ohiopyle and Surrounding Communities, Volume III (2008)

Yesteryear in Ohiopyle and Surrounding Communities, Volume II (1994)

Yesteryear in Ohiopyle and Surrounding Communities, Volume I (1993)

No Outlet! (1993)

Incidents (1992)

Nanny's Kitchen Cookbook (1991)

Natural Remedies, Recipes & Realities (1986)

The Deerhunter's Guide to Success...from the woods to the skillet (1985)

Natural Remedies (1984)

Unforgettable Poems for Everyday People (1984)

What's Happenin' Around Ohiopyle (1981)

www.ohiopyle.info; www.marcimcguinness.com,,

www.positivelypublished.com, www.uniontownspeedway.com

Made in the USA
Charleston, SC
01 June 2014